Zombelina

Kristyn Crow

illustrated by Molly Idle

BLOOMSBURY

NEW YORK LONDON NEW DELHI SYDNEY

For my siblings: Michele, Rob, Janelle, Mike, John-David,
and Jason, who supported me when I was alone and afraid —K. C.

For Chris, post-humorously —M. I.

Text copyright © 2013 by Kristyn Crow
Illustrations copyright © 2013 by Molly Idle

First published in the United States of America in July 2013
by Walker Books for Young Readers, an imprint of Bloomsbury Publishing, Inc.
www.bloomsbury.com

Bloomsbury is a registered trademark of Bloomsbury Publishing Plc

For information about permission to reproduce selections from this book, write to
Permissions, Bloomsbury Children's Books, 1385 Broadway, New York, NY 10018
Bloomsbury books may be purchased for business or promotional use. For information on bulk purchases
please contact Macmillan Corporate and Premium Sales Department at specialmarkets@macmillan.com

Library of Congress Cataloging-in-Publication Data
Crow, Kristyn.
Zombelina / Kristyn Crow, Molly Idle.
p.   cm.
Summary: A young zombie gives a haunting performance at her first ballet dance recital.
ISBN 978-0-8027-2803-6 (hardcover) • ISBN 978-0-8027-2804-3 (reinforced)
[1. Stories in rhyme. 2. Zombies—Fiction. 3. Ballet dancing—Fiction.]
I. Idle, Molly Schaar, illustrator. II. Title.
PZ8.3.C8858Zo 2013   [E]—dc23   2012027333

Art created with Prismacolor pencils on vellum-finish Bristol
Typeset in Franklin Caslon
Book design by Regina Flath

Printed in China by C&C Offset Printing Co., Ltd., Shenzhen, Guangdong
3 5 7 9 10 8 6 4 2 (hardcover)
1 3 5 7 9 10 8 6 4 2 (reinforced)

My name's Zombelina, and I love to dance.
I sway and sashay in a weird zombie trance.

I moonwalk with mummies and boogie with bats.

I wiggle with werewolves and rock out with rats.

I spin like a specter and glide like a ghost.

But I love to dance for my family the most.

We live on the corner of Twisted Tree Lane,
in a creaky old house with a bat weather vane.

My mom can be nitpicky. Dad blows his fuse.
My brother does not close his mouth when he chews.

And me? I amaze them with zombie ballet.
Though sometimes I get a bit carried away.

We all hang together in good times and bad.
I'm glad they're my brother, my mom, and my dad.

One morning my mother said, "Dear Zombelina,
it's time you turned into a REAL ballerina!"

I thought she'd do magic. I thought I'd hear, *POOF!*
But no, we took off from the top of our roof.
We shopped for ballet slippers, tutus, and tights . . .

I started a dance class on Saturday nights.

Madame Maladroit said, "She looks a bit green,
but my, what extension! The best that I've seen!"

My class didn't like me. They cringed at the bar.
They said I was taking my talents too far.

But soon I was learning techniques of ballet.
And I practiced at home in my attic each day.

My demi-pliés made the
spiderwebs tatter.

My wicked chassés made
the skeletons chatter.

The attic floors creaked—
and the mockingbirds shrieked—
as my grand pirouette caused the mirrors to shatter.

I practiced my arabesque night after night.
The werewolves and poltergeists howled with delight!

And then . . .
The day came! My recital was here!
The red curtains parted. I shivered with fear.

The music began, and I pointed my toes.

(*Gulp.*)

The crowd was so QUIET! They stared, and I FROZE!

I started to twitch. I went into a trance.
My class began twirling, but I couldn't dance—

not when nothing was growling . . .
or clanking
or clunking
or rattling
or howling!

I quivered and shivered right down to my bones.
I held out my arms and I made a few moans.
"A ZOMBIE!" the crowd cried with horrified screams.
This wasn't the ballet debut of my dreams.

They all fled the theater.
My classmates left too.
I stood there, alone,
Wondering what I should do.

Until I could hear a familiar **"YOO-HOOOOO!"**
And there was my FAMILY! They finally appeared!

And they shrieked
and they howled
and they snarled
and they cheered!

The seats in the theater filled up once again.
A packed house of SPOOKS! So I breathed and began.

"HOORAY!" called my brother.
"ENCORE!" cried my dad. "You're the
best ballerina this world's ever had!"
My mom said, "Bewitching! So lively and airy—
we're getting the chills! You're so good, it's SCARY!"

Madame Maladroit cried, "BRAVO! MAGNIFIQUE!
My very *best* student! DREAD-fully unique!"

They threw me black roses and clapped for me—WOW!
And I was so proud that I took a big bow.

We flew home together to Twisted Tree Lane,
to our creaky old house with a bat weather vane.

My family surprised me with monster balloons.
We ate spider sundaes with skeleton spoons!

They said my performance was HAUNTING tonight!
My family makes everything turn out all right.
"You sure came ALIVE on the stage!" my mom said . . .

But I was DEAD tired.

YaaaWWWWnnnn.

So I danced off to bed.